So Sleepy Story

Uri Shulevitz

Farrar Straus Giroux · New York

Copyright © 2006 by Uri Shulevitz. All rights reserved. Distributed in Canada
by Douglas & McIntyre Ltd. Color separations by Chroma Graphics PTE Ltd.
Printed and bound in the United States of America by Phoenix Color Corporation.
First edition, 2006
10 9 8 7 6 5 4 3 2 1

www.fsgkidsbooks.com

Library of Congress Cataloging-in-Publication Data
Shulevitz, Uri, date.
    So sleepy story / Uri Shulevitz.— 1st ed.
        p.   cm.
    Summary: A little boy dreams that his house comes alive with dishes that sway,
chairs that rock, and clocks that call "Cuckoo," but when he awakes, all is quiet.
    ISBN-13: 978-0-374-37031-2
    ISBN-10: 0-374-37031-1
    [1. Dreams—Fiction.   2. Sleep—Fiction.]   I. Title.

PZ7.S5594 Sos 2006
[E]—dc22
                                                        2005051146

To the memory of Lyonel Feininger,
whose graphic work inspired some
of the pictures in this book

*I*n a sleepy sleepy house
everything is sleepy sleepy.

Sleepy chairs
by sleepy table
sleepy pictures
on sleepy walls

sleepy cuckoo-clock
by sleepy dishes
on sleepy shelves
and a sleepy cat
on a sleepy chair

and a sleepy sleepy boy
in a sleepy sleepy bed.

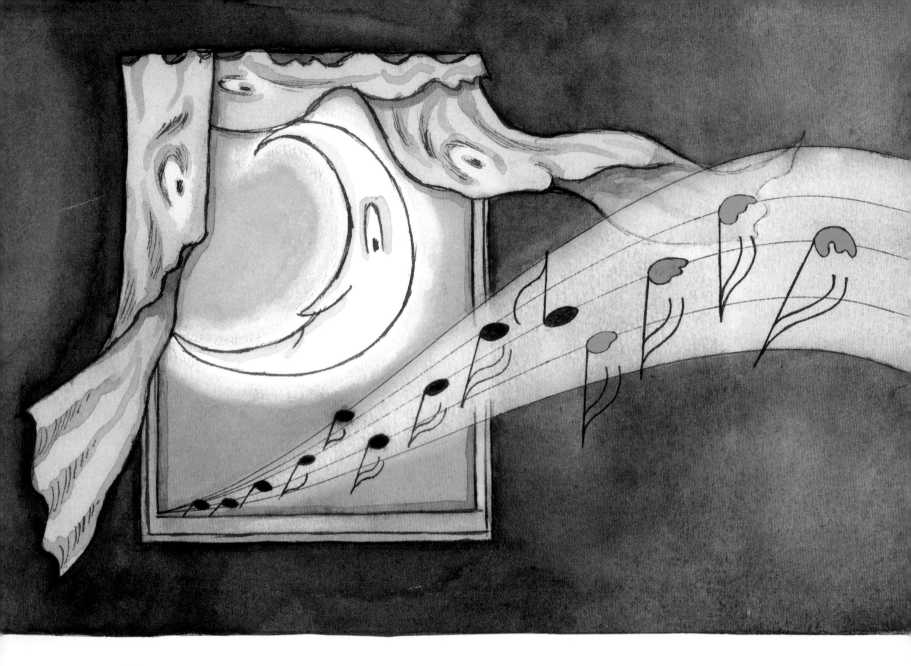

Then
softly softly
music drifts in.

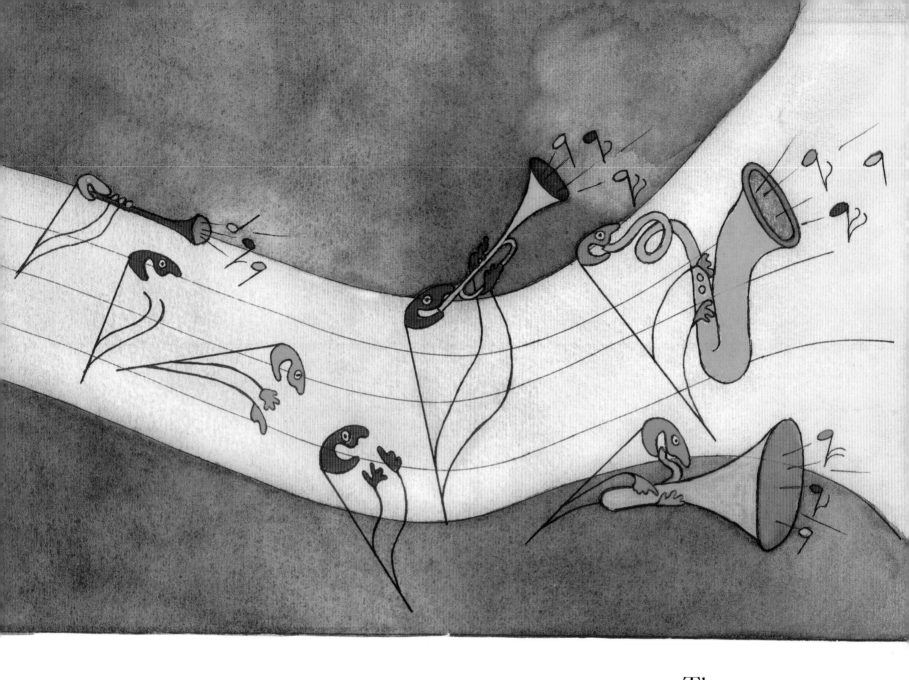

Then
louder
and louder.

Sleepy chairs
begin to shake

then rock.

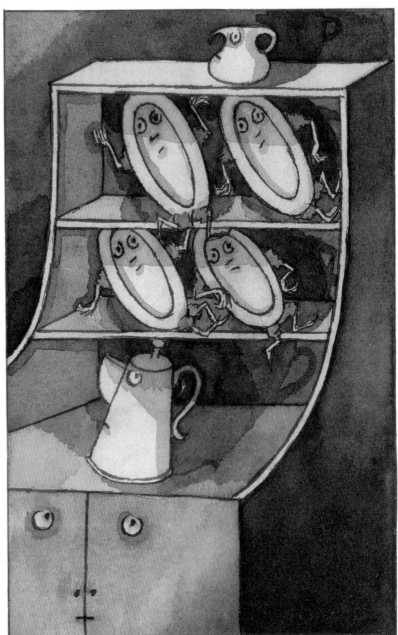

Sleepy dishes
begin to sway

then dance.

Until a dish
rolls off the shelf and

clatters onto the floor
waking sleepy cat.

Cuckoo-clock bird
begins to call
Cuckoo! Cuckoo!

and
sleepy boy opens
his sleepy eyes.

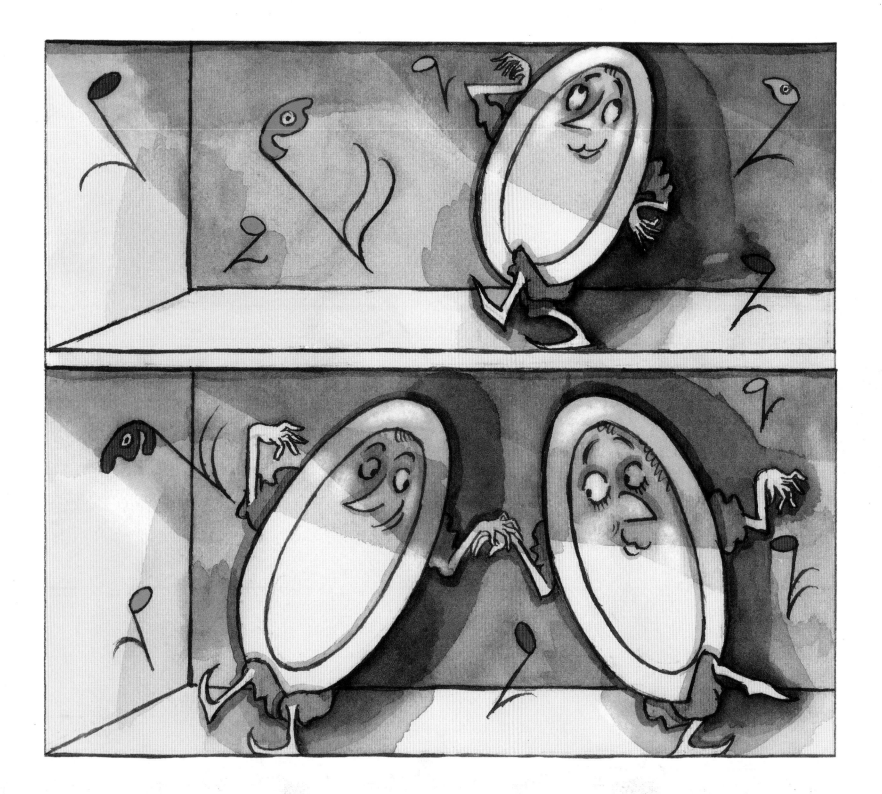

Now

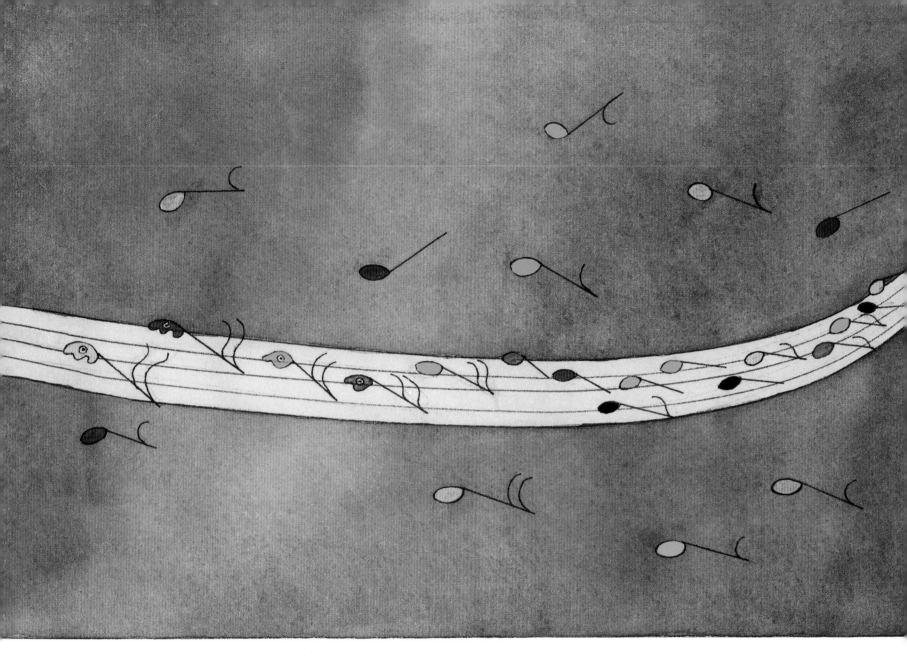

softly softly
music drifts away

cuckoo-clock bird
falls silent

cat shuts its eyes
and all is quiet
again.

And sleepy boy
falls back to sleep

in a sleepy sleepy house

where sleepy pictures
on sleepy walls

and sleepy dishes
on sleepy shelves

are sleepy
sleepy.